Jimmy Finds His Voice

Written by

JAMES DOTI

Illustrated by

LISA MERTINS

Jabberwocky
Books

Dear Reader,

When I was a little boy, other children laughed at me because of the way I spoke. As hard as I tried, I couldn't pronounce certain words correctly.

My mom and dad understood my words. But when children heard me talk, they would laugh and tease me. Their bullying made me mad and sad and lonely, all at the same time. So I tried not to talk in front of other children. It was like I had lost my voice.

Then one day, my mom told me I would soon start attending school as a first grader. Although she said I'd like school, I knew that children there would make fun of me.

On the first day of first grade, my mom and my dog, Blackie, walked me to school. As we got closer and closer, I got more and more nervous. I knew that my familiar world—being at home with my parents, where I didn't have to talk to other kids—was coming to an end.

When we arrived at the school, I stopped to look at the entrance doors. These were not ordinary doors, like the ones on our house. These doors were huge, and they also were kind of scary, because I knew that as soon as I walked through them, I would enter a brand new world.

I hope you enjoy reading about what happened to me as a little boy after I entered my new world. Perhaps it will remind you of the new worlds that you've entered through the doors that have crossed your paths.

Your friend,
Jimmy

Jimmy walks to school with his mom and his best friend—his dog, Blackie—just as he's done every day since he started first grade. In one hand he holds Blackie's leash, while the other carries his Gene Autry cowboy lunch box. Jimmy's mom is wearing a winter hat she knitted for herself. Although Blackie has his red-and-green plaid jacket on, he is shivering from the cold. Jimmy's yellow galoshes crunch the crusty patches of icy snow on the sidewalk. He walks slowly, because he doesn't want to go to school.

"All the kids make fun of me because I don't say my worbs wight. They laugh at me all the time," Jimmy tells his mom.

"I keep saying to you, Jimmy, not to worry about them," his mom replies. "Just be a good boy and listen to everything Mrs. Lyons teaches you."

Mrs. Lyons is Jimmy's first-grade teacher. He likes her. She is nice to him, but she can't stop the other kids from teasing him.

As Jimmy, his mom, and Blackie near the large doors at the entrance to Reinberg School, Jimmy remembers how scared he was when he first entered those doors three months ago. After all this time, he is still scared.

Jimmy kisses his mom and pats Blackie's little head.

"When Blackie and I come to pick you up after school," his mom says, "I'll bring you a chocolate chip cookie."

Even the thought of his favorite cookie doesn't take away Jimmy's feeling of being scared. Very reluctantly and very slowly, he walks toward the doors of the school. As he struggles to pull one of the heavy doors open, he turns his head around to take one more look at his mom and Blackie.

Jimmy's mom smiles and waves good-bye.

Jimmy knows her smile is a sad smile. He knows that his mom is sad because he is sad.

Jimmy goes to his locker. The metal door squeaks as he yanks it open. He takes off his hat, scarf, and heavy winter coat and shoves them all inside. He bends down to unclip the buckles of his rubber galoshes. Then he peels them off and tosses them into the locker.

Mrs. Lyons greets him in the hallway outside the classroom. "Good morning, James," she says cheerfully.

"Goob morning," Jimmy replies.

Jimmy knows he said "goob" when he tried to say "good," and that makes him feel even sadder. He lowers his head and silently walks into the classroom and sits down at his desk. Jimmy's friend Mary Ambrose is already seated at the desk next to him. Johnny Redstone and Adam McCormick plop down noisily at the desks behind them.

"Ha! Jimmy doesn't know how to say 'Good morning!'" Adam shouts out. Johnny joins Adam in laughing at Jimmy.

Mary doesn't like it when the other kids make fun of Jimmy, so she gives Johnny and then Adam mean-looking stares.

The class quickly comes to order as Mrs. Lyons starts to speak. Jimmy notices that she is holding a book behind her.

"Well, girls and boys," Mrs. Lyons says, "I have a surprise for you. We are going to perform a student play on the stage of the assembly hall. Your family and friends can all come to see it. The play is based on a fairy tale—'The Elves and the Shoemaker.'"

Turning around, Mrs. Lyons places the book on her desk. She picks up a piece of chalk and writes the names—"Jakob and Wilhelm Grimm"—on the blackboard.

"These two brothers wrote 'The Elves and the Shoemaker' more than a hundred years ago," says Mrs. Lyons. "You know some of the other stories they wrote, like 'Snow White,' 'Hansel and Gretel,' and 'Cinderella.'

"'The Elves and the Shoemaker' begins a long time ago in a two-storied gabled home where a shoemaker and his wife live and work. In his workshop, the shoemaker wearily cut leather all day to make a pair of shoes. By the time he'd cut all the pieces for the shoes, he was too tired to sew them together. So he and his wife ate their soup and went to bed."

Opening her eyes wider, Mrs. Lyons goes on with the story. "That night, four little elves with long, pointy ears quietly crawled through the window of the shoemaker's workshop. They were wearing ragged clothes and had no shoes. They were so cold, the first thing they did was huddle and warm up around the still-hot glowing embers of the stove."

Mrs. Lyons then picks up the book from her desk. She opens it and begins to read:

"*This place feels so warm and cozy*," said one of the elves.

"*If we stay here tonight and come back again, we must do something nice in return*," said another one of the elves.

"*I have an idea. Let's help the shoemaker by finishing the shoes he's making*," said another elf.

"*Now that's a good idea*," said the littlest elf.

Mrs. Lyons looks up from the book. "And that's what they did."

Mrs. Lyons continues telling the story. "The next morning the shoemaker and his wife woke up to find the leather pieces sewn together into a beautiful pair of shoes. They wondered if the shoes were made by some sort of magic. But magic or not, they were very pleased."

"All day the shoemaker cut leather for another pair of shoes. It was too late to sew the leather together, so he and his wife ate their soup and then trudged up the steps to go to bed."

Mrs. Lyons then asks, "What do you think happens next?"

Mary Ambrose raises her hand and says, "I bet the elves sneak into the shoemaker's workshop again to get warm and sew another pair of shoes."

"That's right, Mary," Mrs. Lyons replies. "And they go back the next night and the next night, getting all warm and cozy while sewing the shoes for the shoemaker.

"By that time, the shoemaker and his wife began to suspect that the shoes were not being made by magic," explains Mrs. Lyons.

Picking up the book to show the illustration, Mrs. Lyons continues. "So later that evening, they hid behind a door and peeked out to find out what was going on. They didn't wait long before they were astonished to see the four little barefoot elves crawl through the window. They watched all night as the elves warmed up by the stove and then went to work at sewing the shoes. Just before sunrise, the shoes were finished, and the elves crawled back out of the window."

Mrs. Lyons again starts to read from the book:

"So that explains the mystery," said the shoemaker's wife.

"Oh, we must do something for those hardworking elves," replied the shoemaker.

"I have an idea," said the wife. "I'll make new clothes, and you make new shoes for them. I'll even bake some of my special meat pies."

"Now that's a good idea," said the shoemaker.

Mrs. Lyons closes the book and clutches it close to her as she continues telling the story.

"The next night, the elves entered the shop, shivering from the cold outside. But instead of pieces of leather waiting for them they found new clothes, shoes, and piping-hot meat pies. As the elves started to sniff hungrily at the spicy nutmeg smell of the meat pies, the shoemaker and his wife came out from behind the door.

"They told the elves they were very pleased by their hard work, and wanted to show their appreciation for a job well done.

"The hungry elves quickly dressed up in their new clothes and shoes, so they could get to devouring the meat pies."

"Let's see how the story ends," Mrs. Lyons says. She opens the book and reads the last page:

The shoemaker said to the elves, "I have an idea. Why don't you come every night? I will leave the cut leather for you to sew the shoes. In return for your hard work, we will mend your clothes and shoes and make sure we always have meat pies waiting for you."

"Now that's a good idea," said the littlest of the elves.

Then the elves joined together at the table with the steaming meat pies on plates in front of them and happily sang:

> *"We love to sing our song.*
>
> *We sew shoes all night long.*
>
> *Meat pies in our tummy*
>
> *Taste so warm and yummy."*

Mrs. Lyons closes the book and sets it down on her desk. "Well, class, what do you think of the story?"

Mrs. Lyons' questions always scare Jimmy. He never raises his hand to answer for fear that the other kids will laugh at him. But he need not have been afraid. Other children are shouting out answers.

"I like the meat pies," says Adam.

"I like the cute little elves," says Mary.

"I like the part about the elves not wearing shoes," says Johnny.

"Well, John," Mrs. Lyons replies, "you're going to find out what it's like not wearing shoes, because I want you to be one of the elves in our play."

Johnny gulps in response.

"And I'd like Adam McCormick to play the shoemaker and Mary Ambrose to be his wife," Mrs. Lyons announces.

Adam's and Mary's cheeks turn red in embarrassment that they will be a husband and wife.

"Finally," Mrs. Lyons continues, "I'd like Neil Jackson, April Nemick, and James Doti to play the other elves, along with John."

"Oh, no!" Johnny cries out. "Not Doti! He'll ruin the play."

"Yeah," says Adam, "no one will understand him."

Jimmy slides down in his chair, trying to hide from Johnny and Adam, who are pointing fingers and laughing at him. He hears Mrs. Lyons, though, as she says, "I know James will do just fine."

The first thing Jimmy sees as he walks out the school's large doors is his mom and Blackie waiting for him. When Blackie spots Jimmy, his tail starts whipping back and forth.

As Jimmy gets closer, his mom lets go of Blackie's leash and the little dog runs to greet him.

Jimmy picks up Blackie. "Hey, boy, dib you miss me?"

Blackie covers Jimmy's face with wet doggy kisses.

"I missed you, too, Blackie," Jimmy says.

Jimmy's mom hugs him and takes out of her purse the chocolate chip cookie that she had promised him.

Doggy smooches and the chocolate chip cookie help take Jimmy's mind off his newest worry about being cast as an elf in the student play. But he is rudely reminded of it just a moment later, when Johnny runs by him and shouts, "You're going to ruin our play!" Then Johnny turns around and laughs at Jimmy.

"What was that all about?" asks Jimmy's mom.

Jimmy doesn't answer. All he can do is bow his head so his mom can't see the tears burning in his eyes.

Later, at home, wearing his comfy yellow pajamas, Jimmy walks into his mom's hat room. This is the room where his mom turns plain hats into beautiful hats by adding decorations, like ribbons, flowers, veils, and feathers. She places a black hat with a long feather up on a shelf with the other finished hats that she will sell to a nearby hat shop.

Jimmy likes watching his mom decorate the hats. He feels safe in her hat room. He can almost forget about kids laughing at him and making him feel different and dumb.

Suddenly, his mom asks, "Are you ready now to talk about what's troubling you?"

After a long pause, Jimmy answers, "Mrs. Lyons wamps me to be an elf in a school play."

"Why, that's wonderful, Jimmy!" his mom says excitedly. "You will get to be on stage and be an actor."

"But all the kids think I'll mess up the worbs and woom the play."

"Mrs. Lyons doesn't think you'll ruin it," his mom says. "She has confidence in you; otherwise, she wouldn't have picked you. If you do your best, you'll do just fine. The little mistakes aren't important. Now, tell me what the play is all about."

As Jimmy tells his mom the story of "The Elves and the Shoemaker," Blackie is curled up in his little red bed, listening to every word.

A few weeks later, Mrs. Lyons is scurrying back and forth, giving directions to the students as they practice the final scene in the play.

"OK, Adam," Mrs. Lyons says, "now you can say your line."

Acting as the shoemaker, Adam steps forward with confidence and says, "For your hard work, we will make sure we always have hot and juicy meat pies for you."

"Excellent, Adam," says Mrs. Lyons. "Now it's your turn, James."

The elves are all huddled together, looking like scared sheep.

"Come on, James," Mrs. Lyons directs, "you need to step out so everyone can see you."

Slowly, Jimmy places his right foot forward and then his left. He stares at Mrs. Lyons and feels like he is going to be sick.

"No, James, don't look at me," says Mrs. Lyons. "You need to look at the audience when you say your line." She points at the empty seats in the assembly hall. "Imagine that the chairs are all filled with people."

Although Jimmy knows the line, he is afraid to say it.

Finally, with his face reddening and hands in his pockets, Jimmy gulps loudly and says softly, "Now that's a goob idea."

At that, everyone on the stage, except for Mrs. Lyons and Mary, starts laughing at Jimmy.

The next day, when the school bell rings to signal the end of class, Mrs. Lyons asks Jimmy to wait. He stays seated as his classmates run noisily and happily out of the room. When everyone else is gone, he slowly stands and approaches his teacher's desk.

"I'm sorry, James, that some of your classmates laughed at you yesterday," says Mrs. Lyons. "I want you to know that I think you're doing just fine."

"But I don't say the worbs wight," moans Jimmy. "I'm going to woom the play."

"You're not going to ruin the play. In fact, unlike the other actors, you already know all your lines and even where to stand on the stage."

"But the people womp understand me."

"Yes, they will, James. Remember, it's not only what you say that's important. How you say it is important, too. You have to say your words with verve."

"What's… werb?" asks Jimmy.

"Well, James, yesterday I was looking out the classroom window and saw you greet your little dog."

"Yeah, that's my dog, Blackie," says Jimmy.

Mrs. Lyons nods. "I couldn't hear what you said to Blackie, but I could tell from your actions that it was something like, 'Hi, Blackie. I missed you.'"

"That's wight," replies a surprised Jimmy.

"That's what I mean by verve. It's not just the words coming out of your mouth. People also understand by watching what your body is saying." Then, while wagging her finger at him, Mrs. Lyons says, "Remember that, James!"

Later that evening, while watching his mom make hats, Jimmy tries to explain what Mrs. Lyons said to him after school.

As Jimmy's mom listens, she works on adding a blue bow to decorate a hat she is finishing up. "I agree with Mrs. Lyons," she says. "You can't just mouth the words."

"What do you mean?" asks Jimmy.

"What I mean is that you have to use your hands, your face, and your body to express yourself in a lively way."

"I don't understam," answers Jimmy.

"I know that," says his mom. "I can tell you don't understand by the way you're squinting your eyes and pressing your lips together."

Jimmy doesn't say anything, but he realizes his mom is right. He is squinting his eyes and scrunching up his mouth.

Suddenly, his mom points her finger upward and says excitedly, "I have an idea! Let's practice the lines in your play."

But Jimmy is not listening. Instead, his eyes focus on the way his mom raises her arm when she exclaims, "I have an idea!"

When the night of the play arrives, the elves are dressed in the raggedy elves' outfits that Jimmy's mom made for them. They look funny wearing the long, pointy ears she placed over their real ears.

Peeking from behind the curtain, being careful not to step on each other's bare feet, the four elves watch people entering the assembly hall. Jimmy sees his mom, dad, and "nonna"—his grandmother—take their seats.

"Hey, you little elves. Stop peeking!" exclaims Mrs. Lyons. "The play is about to begin."

As Jimmy and the elves rush offstage, the choir takes its place behind the curtain. The curtain rises, and the choir starts to sing the opening song. Then the shoemaker and his wife walk onto the stage.

From the side of the stage, Jimmy sees Adam wearing his shoemaker costume. He is cutting brown cloth that is meant to look like real leather. Jimmy hardly recognizes Mary as the shoemaker's wife. Her curly brown hair is hidden by a gray wig styled into a big bun at the back of her head. She is stirring a pot of pretend soup on top of a stove that has flames painted on it to look like a real fire. Adam and Mary say their lines and walk off the stage.

Then Mrs. Lyons pushes the elves forward, whispering, "Now!"

Hurrying onto the stage, Johnny says, "This place feels warm and cozy."

Then Neil exclaims, "I have an idea! Let's help the shoemaker finish the shoes he's making."

Jimmy knows it's his turn to speak. He takes a deep breath. Then he lifts his arms and stretches them out from his sides. After hesitating for a moment, he says, "Now that's a goob idea."

Jimmy knows he didn't say "good." But no one laughs at him, not even Johnny. Jimmy hears applause from the audience as he and his fellow elves walk off the stage.

"Well done, elves. And I like the way you used verve, Jimmy," Mrs. Lyons says as she winks at him. "But it's not over yet. You still have your final scene."

Jimmy and the elves quickly run back on the stage, where they see new clothes, shoes, and meat pies waiting for them. Suddenly, Adam and Mary jump from behind the door and tell the elves they made all this for them in appreciation of their hard work.

The elves run behind a door to put on their beautiful new clothes and shoes. Then they hurry back out on stage to pretend they are hungrily devouring the meat pies.

The shoemaker and his wife walk over to the elves and ask them to come back every night to sew the shoes. Mary says, "In return, we will mend your new clothes and shoes and have hot and juicy meat pies for you to eat."

That line is Jimmy's cue. He sets down his meat pie, gets up from the table, and walks to the center of the stage. He opens his eyes as wide as he can. He looks out at the audience and sees his mom looking intently at him.

Jimmy sharply raises his right hand, points his finger to the rafters, and exclaims loudly and with verve, "Now that's a goob idea!" At that moment, the audience leaps to its feet, clapping and cheering and laughing. But Jimmy can tell it's the nice kind of laughing—not the bullying kind—and the sparkle in his eyes makes it clear that his smile is a real smile —not the fake kind—as he gazes out at the audience.

After the play, Adam, Mary, Johnny, Neil, and April, still wearing their costumes, come to Jimmy's house for a celebration. Mrs. Lyons comes, too. Blackie's nose twitches with anticipation as it catches the scents coming from the snacks Jimmy's nonna is making.

"Well, Jimmy," his mother says, "I guess Mrs. Lyons was right about using verve."

Johnny asks, "What's all this stuff about verve?"

Mrs. Lyons responds, "It's what James used when he spoke his lines. He brought spirit to the words. He found his voice."

Jimmy is still amazed that no one made fun of him. Maybe his mom and Mrs. Lyons were right when they told him, "Always do your best. If you do, the little mistakes aren't important."

Turning his attention to Adam and Mary, Johnny shouts out, "Hey, Mr. and Mrs. Shoemaker, how about some of those meat pies you're supposed to give us every night?"

Just then, Jimmy sees Nonna carrying a platter piled high with piping hot meat pies. As everyone watches in amazement, the elves know exactly what to do. They get up in an instant, join together in a circle, and start twirling around while singing.

Yipping happily, little Blackie sings right along.

"We love to sing our song.
We sew shoes all night long.
Meat pies in our tummy
Taste so warm and yummy."

From Jimmy to You

There they are—those big scary doors. It was sixty years ago that I first entered those doors and walked into a strange and scary new world.

Now, standing in front of those doors again after so many years, they don't look so big or scary at all. But they still appear to hold some kind of magic, for as I walk through them, it seems like a part of my past comes into view, reawakening distant, gauzy memories:

Memories of Mrs. Lyons greeting me in front of my first-grade classroom. Memories of stuffing galoshes in my locker on cold, snowy days. Memories of standing on a stage, barefoot and wearing funny-looking clothes and pointy ears. And a memory of finding my voice.

I walk over to that stage and place myself on the same spot where I stood as a child. Looking out on an empty assembly hall, I imagine an audience. I see my mom, dad, and nonna looking at me. Then I raise my right hand, point my finger to the rafters, and say with as much verve as I can muster,

"Now that's a good idea!"

The Shoemaker's Wife's Meat Pies

1 tablespoon olive oil
½ cup chopped onion
½ cup raisins
½ teaspoon nutmeg
¾ pound lean ground beef
2 sheets refrigerated pie dough
1 egg mixed with 1 teaspoon of water for egg wash

Preheat the oven to 400°. Spray a baking pan with non-stick spray.

Heat olive oil in a frying pan on range over medium temperature.

Then add the onion, raisins and nutmeg, and cook, stirring until the onion softens.

Add the ground beef and continue cooking and stirring until the meat browns. Add salt and pepper to taste.

Remove from heat and allow to cool.

Roll out the dough and cut it into 4-inch circles.

Top each dough circle with a heaping tablespoon of the meat mixture.

Brush around the edge of the dough circles with egg wash; then fold in half. Use a fork to press the edges together to seal the meat pie.

Brush the top of the meat pies with egg wash and place in baking pan.

Bake for 18 minutes or until the dough is golden brown.

Final Step: When the meat pies are cool, find a cozy place and munch away at them while reading this book.

Dedicated with respect and gratitude
to Mrs. Lyons and all the teachers
who helped me find my voice.
J.D.

To the children that talk, walk, think or do things differently,
I was once where you are now.
The best part is, I still am!
L.M.

We gratefully acknowledge
the invaluable editorial and design assistance
provided by Ann Cameron.

Jabberwocky Press
212 3rd Avenue North, Suite 290
Minneapolis, MN 55401
612.455.2293
www.Jabberwocky-Books.com

Ordering information for retailers/libraries/wholesalers:
Itasca Books
800.901.3480
www.itascabooks.com

ISBN - 978-1-935204-47-3
ISBN - 2012945965

Editorial and Design Assistance by Ann Cameron
Cover Design and Typeset by Kristeen Ott

Printed in the United States of America